GUS and GRANDPA and the Christmas Cookies

Claudia Mills ★ Pictures by Catherine Stock

A Sunburst Book
Farrar, Straus and Giroux

To all the men and women
who ring the bells
and tend the kettles

—C.M.

For Felix and Ted

—C.S.

Distributed in Canada by Douglas & McIntyre Ltd.
Color separations by Berryville Graphics/All Systems Color
Printed in the United States of America
First edition, 1997
Sunburst edition, 2000
1 3 5 7 9 10 8 6 4 2

Library of Congress Cataloging-in-Publication Data
Mills, Claudia.
Gus and Grandpa and the Christmas cookies / Claudia Mills ; illustrated by Catherine Stock. — 1st ed.
p. cm.
Summary: Having baked six dozen Christmas cookies for themselves and been given many more by the neighbors, Gus and Grandpa find a rewarding solution to disposing of their extra holiday treats.
ISBN: 0-374-42815-8 (pbk.)
[1. Cookies—Fiction. 2. Baking—Fiction. 3. Christmas—Fiction. 4. Grandfathers—Fiction.] I. Stock, Catherine, ill. II. Title.
PZ7.M63963Gv 1997
[E]—dc20 96-31254

Contents

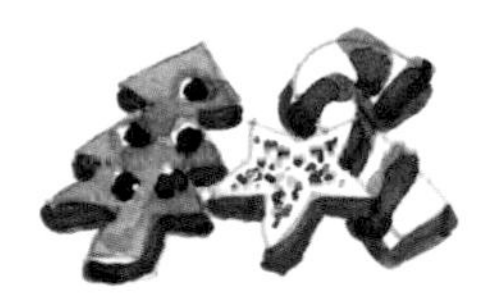

Busy Baking

Christmas was coming!
Gus and Grandpa
were baking cookies
at Grandpa's house.
Gus watched as Grandpa
rolled out the cookie dough
with a heavy wooden rolling pin.

The dough stuck
to the counter.
"Hey!" Grandpa said
to the dough.
"Stop that sticking!"
Gus sprinkled more flour
on the counter.
Grandpa sprinkled more flour
on the rolling pin.
Outside the window,
the snow was falling
like flour sifted
from the sky.

The dough stuck again.
"No more sticking!"
Gus shouted.
It was fun yelling
at the cookie dough.

Grandpa cut out stars
and Christmas trees
and reindeer.
Gus ate the scraps
of leftover dough.

Grandpa cut out bells
and Santas
and candy canes.
Gus ate more scraps
of dough.

Gus's mother and father
never gave Gus
raw dough to eat.
But Grandpa liked
eating dough, too.
So did Grandpa's dog,
Skipper.

Grandpa's oven was old,
just like Grandpa.
He had to light it
with a wooden match.
Grandpa put the first trays
of cookies in the oven.
Gus set the timer
for ten minutes.
Then he and Grandpa waited
for the scent
of fresh-baked cookies
to fill the air
in Grandpa's house
with the smell
of Christmas.

The Red Kettle

"Oh, no," Grandpa said
when it was time
to frost the cookies.
"I forgot to buy the sprinkles.
We can't have Christmas cookies
without sprinkles."
Gus and Grandpa
drove to the store.

Outside the store,
a man dressed as Santa Claus
stood next to a red kettle.
He was ringing a bell.
Some people stopped
and dropped money
into the red kettle.
"God bless you,"

the man said to them.
Gus was surprised.
None of the people
had sneezed.
But then he understood.
The man was saying
a prayer
to thank the people.

Inside the store,
Gus and Grandpa bought sprinkles
and colored sugar
and tiny red and green
candy stars.
When they left the store,
the man with the red kettle
was still ringing his bell.

Gus tugged on Grandpa's sleeve.
"Why are people
putting money in there?"
Gus asked Grandpa.

"The man will give
the money in the kettle
to children who don't have
enough food to eat
or warm clothes to wear
or toys for Christmas,"
Grandpa said.

Gus reached into his pocket.
Grandpa had given him
two shiny new quarters,
left over from the shopping.
"May I give the man
my quarters?"
Gus asked.
Grandpa nodded.

Then Gus felt shy.
He didn't know
if two quarters
was the right amount
to put in the kettle.
A woman wearing a blue coat
put a dollar
in the kettle.
"God bless you,"
the man told her.

He kept on
ringing his bell.
Would the man say
"God bless you"
to Gus, too?

"Go on," Grandpa said.
He gave Gus
a gentle nudge.
Gus walked forward.
He dropped his quarters
into the kettle
one by one.

"God bless you,"
the man told him.

Gus ran back to Grandpa.
He took Grandpa's hand.
He hoped his quarters
would buy other children
some Christmas cookies
with sprinkles
and colored sugar
and tiny red and green
candy stars
on top.

Too Many Cookies

Back home again,
Gus and Grandpa frosted the cookies
with red and green and white frosting.
They put the decorations
all over them.
It took a long time.
Finally the cookies
were done.
Gus had never seen
such beautiful cookies.

Then the doorbell rang.
Gus went with Grandpa
to answer it.
It was Mrs. Wrenn,
who lived next door
in the blue house.
"I brought you
a couple dozen cookies,"
Mrs. Wrenn said.
"I thought a man alone
would like some
home baking!"
Grandpa thanked Mrs. Wrenn.
He did not tell her
that he already had
six dozen cookies
spread out on his kitchen table.

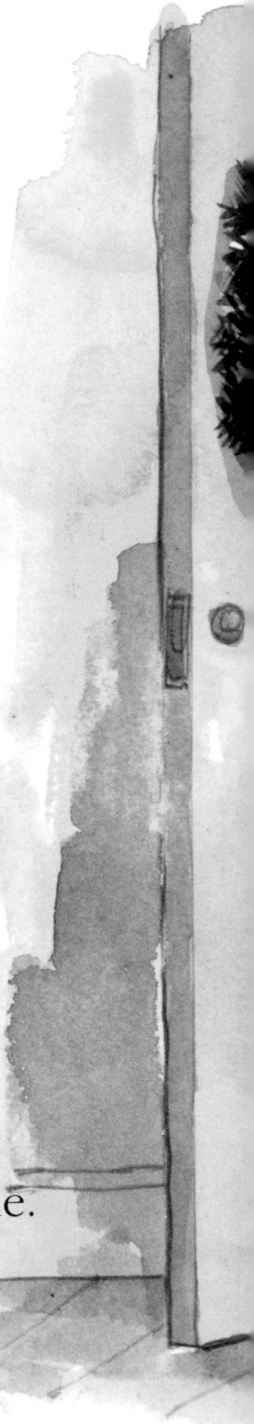

Ten minutes later,
the doorbell rang again.
It was Mrs. Perry,
who lived next door
in the brown house.
"I've been baking
Christmas cookies,"
Mrs. Perry said.
"I baked an extra
two dozen just for you."
Grandpa thanked Mrs. Perry.
He did not tell her
that he already had
six dozen cookies
on his kitchen table,
plus two dozen cookies
from Mrs. Wrenn.

Gus and Grandpa
were just sitting down
to sample their cookies
when the doorbell rang
a third time.

SUGA
DROSTE
CACAO

It was Mrs. Tucker,
who lived behind Grandpa
in the gray house.
"It's cookie time!"
Mrs. Tucker said.
"You have to have
some home-baked cookies
at Christmas!"
Grandpa thanked Mrs. Tucker

for *her* two dozen cookies.
He did not tell her
that he already had
six dozen cookies
on his kitchen table,
plus two dozen cookies
from Mrs. Wrenn
and two dozen cookies
from Mrs. Perry.

After Mrs. Tucker left,
Gus and Grandpa
looked at each other.
"I guess those good ladies
don't figure that
a man can bake,"
Grandpa said.
"What are we going to do
with all these cookies, Gus?
How many dozen cookies
can one man and one boy eat?"

“God Bless You”

What *could* they do
with twelve dozen cookies?
Gus tried to think.
They could give some
to Gus’s parents.
But Gus’s mother
liked to bake
her own cookies.
They could feed some
cookies to Skipper.
Skipper liked cookies.
But he liked bones more.

Gus thought and thought.
Suddenly he had an idea.
"Do you think
the man with the red kettle
would give our cookies
to the same children
who are getting my quarters?"

"Let's go find out,"
Grandpa said.

Gus helped Grandpa
put the cookies they had made
in a great big pile
in a cardboard box.

Then Gus and Grandpa
drove back to the store.
It was growing dark,

but the man with the red kettle
was still outside,
ringing his bell.

"Could you use
six dozen fresh-baked
homemade Christmas cookies?"
Grandpa asked him.

"I sure could,"
the man said.
"I will take them down
to the Christmas party
at the homeless shelter tonight."

Gus and Grandpa brought
the big box of cookies
from the car.
"Here they are,"
Gus said to the man.

"God bless you,"
the man said
to Gus and Grandpa.

Gus felt warm inside,
even though it was still snowing.

Then Gus and Grandpa
drove home together
past twinkling Christmas lights
shining brightly
through the falling snow.